LOST CAT

BY TAD HARDY
ILLUSTRATED BY DAVID GOLDIN

Houghton Mifflin Company / Boston 1996

For information about this and other Houghton Mifflin
trade and reference books and multimedia products,
visit The Bookstore at Houghton Mifflin on the World Wide
Web at http://www.hmco.com/trade/.

Manufactured in the United States of America

The text of this book is set in 20-point Berliner Grotesk Demi Bold.
The illustrations are watercolor and ink, reproduced in full color.

WOZ   10   9   8   7   6   5   4   3   2   1

LIBRARY OF CONGRESS CATALOGING-IN-PUBLICATION DATA
Hardy, Tad.
Lost cat / by Tad Hardy ; illustrated by David Goldin.   p. cm.
Summary: A cat owner lovingly describes the habits and appearance
of his beloved lost pet, hoping that someone will return him, while the
person who found him views the very same cat quite differently.
ISBN 0-395-73574-2
[1. Cats—Fiction. 2. Lost and found possessions—Fiction.
3. Stories in rhyme.] I. Goldin, David, ill. II. Title.
PZ8.3.H1996Lo 1996
[E]—dc20   94-23974
CIP   AC

FOR ELLIOT AND HIS MOM

—T. H.

TO STEPHANIE EMMA

—D. G.

Lost cat.
Where's he at?

Plump and soft.
Loves to chat.

Black stripes,
Whiskers white.
Nose is pink.
Has an overbite.

**Prim and proud.
Enjoys a crowd.**

Sits in laps
When he's allowed.

Loves to eat.
Shares your seat.

Snuggles tight
Around your feet.

Miss him dearly.
Want him back.
Oh please help me
FIND MY CAT!

Cat found.
Fat...
And round.
Black stripes running
Up and down.

Huge pink nose.
Whiskers light.
Some are missing,
Some are white.

Sleeps all day.
Meows all night.
Teeth stick out
And don't bite right.

Jumped and shouted,
Whistled and clapped.
Cannot get him
Off my lap.

Swiped my dinner.
Knocked me flat.
Someone please
COME GET THIS CAT!

Cat will be there,
But not me.
Snitched my breakfast.
Drank my tea.

Stole my seat.
Drew a crowd.

I haven't slept...
He meows too loud!

Cat is back!
Safe and sound!
Seems just fine,
Still soft and round.

Meows to greet me.
Hugs my feet.

Curls beside me
When I eat.

Warms my lap.
Shares my day.
Stripes and whiskers
Home to stay.

Missed him dearly.
Thrilled he's back.
Who could live
Without this cat?

Hardy, Tad. SEP   1996

Lost cat.

H
A

DATE			